ALICE AND HER PUP

By
Norman Hecht

Copyright © 2024

Norman Hecht

ISBN

978-1-964656-30-4

978-1-964656-31-1

978-1-964656-32-8

All Rights Reserved. Any unauthorized reprint or use of this material is strictly prohibited. No part of this book may be reproduced or transmitted in any form or by any means, electronic or mechanical, including photocopying, recording, or by any information storage and retrieval system without express written permission from the author.

All reasonable attempts have been made to verify the accuracy of the information provided in this publication. Nevertheless, the author assumes no responsibility for any errors and/or omissions.

DEDICATION

To Annie, my mom, whom I lost at age five, likely the source of my spirit and drive.
To Elaine, my wife, ever at my side,
matriarch of our loving hive.
To my children, Sharon, Ken, and Laura, who inspired my life and will to strive.
To my grandchildren, Sarah, Elana, Ben, Sammy, and Nikki the bountiful harvest of my life.
And finally to Billie Eden, enchanting and bright, filling each day with joy and delight.

A lass named Alice
Lived not in a palace.
Just a modest little home
With a roof, not a dome.

She was nine years old
Very sweet; not bold.
She was happy not sad
And very rarely bad.

She had a mom and a dad
And Alice made them glad.
She was trusting and kind
And always did mind
What her folks did say
When in the street she did play.

On a cold wintry morning
An hour past dawning
Alice went out
to walk about.

The snow had stopped falling
and the winds began stalling
as Alice commenced calling
to a pup sliding and crawling.

The pup was all muddy
And so so cruddy

And Alice felt sad
As she called to her dad

Seeing the pup
Wandering around
Scratching the ground
A rough-looking hound
Making nary a sound

Her dad came to look.
In the moment it took
What came to his mind
Was the pup was blind.

Dad told his daughter
That no one had lost her.
The dog had no home
Needed a wash and a comb.

Alice walked over to touch
Her affection so much.
She felt for its struggle
It needed a huggle.

A neighbor looked out
And harshly did shout.
A mean hostile yell
So Alice's eyes teared well.
"It's not a good mutt
So my door I did shut."

"Leave him alone."
"Don't give him a bone."
"I want him away."
"He cannot here stay."

"I shooed him out
and don't you dare pout.
He cannot here sleep
And you cannot him keep."

He always got lost
So out he was tossed.
He once found my shoe
And eagerly did chew.

"He has no sight
Not even in light.
And angry in spite
He attacked and did bite.
And gave me much fright."

"I am sure that he knew
That he should not that do.
Never never to do
as old as he grew."

"I gave him my boot
And don't give a hoot.
Don't go near that cur
Don't touch his fur."

"You'll see he's not nice
And has many a vice.
He's blind as a bat
Not wise as my cat."

The more Alice could hear
She felt tender and dear
Wanted ever to care
For that puppy so near.

She called to her dad.
Please, please, don't be mad
I'm so very glad
This pup can be had.

I want him to keep
and to cuddle at sleep.
I'll give him a name
Not silly or lame.
His name will be Bert
Cause it rhymes with his hurt.
And when I call Bert.
He'll be so alert

To the sound of my voice
He'll have no choice
But to pay heed to my call
And not run into the wall

He will listen and learn
Avoiding fire and burn.
I'll feed him
And lead him
And protect him from harm
You'll see he'll have charm

So please tell the lady
Dark eyed and shady
We'll buy the hound
To keep safe and sound.

Bert will stay off her ground
And not be around
To disturb or
Perturb

Dad said he'd take Bert home
No longer let loose to roam.
And Bert learned anew
A loving family and knew
A love that was true
With nothing to rue.

A year went by
With nary a sigh.
Alice and Bert
Pleasant unhurt

A girl and her pup
Cheered each other up.
The neighbor mean
Remained quite unseen

Until the day
That was far from play.
'Twas late at night
And all seemed right.

The family asleep
No sounds, not a peep
When out of the blue
Without much ado
Bert yelped in the dark
And then a loud bark

Bert ran to the door
And scratched at the floor.
Alice awake with a shake
Raced quickly to make
Bert soothed and calm
But then smelled smoke
Got the family awoke

The smoke and the smell
And fire flickering well
Came from next door
That neighbor once more

Alice's dad got the phone
And groaned with a moan
As he dialed nine one one
And soon was done
Getting help to run
To douse the fire
A danger most dire.

The fire truck came
The police the same
An ambulance too
A full fledged crew.

Soon the fire subdued
Lit a much better mood.
The neighbor was saved
Happily she waved
Her joy at being unhurt
To the dog named Bert.

Who saved her life
And had suffered her strife
She hugged sweet Bert
And was sorry for the hurt
She had done to him
Her memory not dim.

The pup so sweet
Yelped kindly at her feet
No anger no fear
All good over here
A sorrowful tear
From the lady dear

She hugged the mutt
To her belly and gut
And begged it to forgive
Now that her life she could live.
And that is the story of
Alice and her pup
I hope it serves to cheer you up.

THE END

www.ingramcontent.com/pod-product-compliance
Lightning Source LLC
LaVergne TN
LVHW070436080526
838202LV00034B/2652